CHILDREN OF THE NIGHT

a tragedy in five acts

WRITTEN AND ILLUSTRATED BY GUY DAVIS

cover painting by Vince Locke

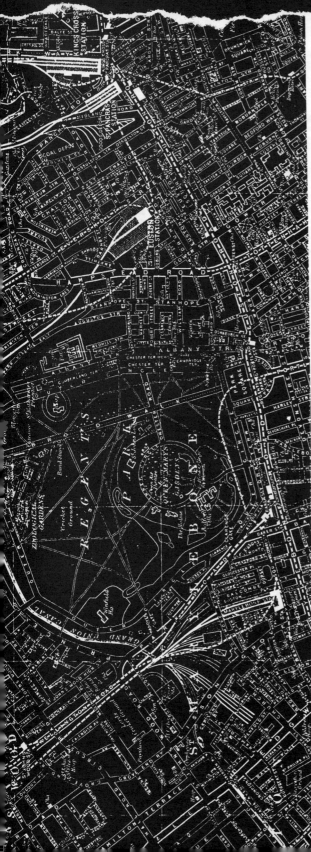

Introduction

Baker Street, the name conjures up many images, mainly of an old Victorian London and residence of Sherlock Holmes. You won't find Sir Arthur Conan Doyle's slueths here though, just some similarities and a little bit more. A mystery of gaslight and mohawks set in an England where World War II never happened and the Victorian era is resurrected into present day values. All of which is only a backdrop for the mysteries and a setting to clash with London's punk sub-culture. And basically that's what this book is supposed to be, a punk mystery (or at least what punk used to be). If i' strives to be anything it's to be different and hopefully it is.

Guy Davis

When creators embark on a project, they are never sure how much their created worlc will open up and lend itself to a view unexpected. On Baker Street, we have seen the focus spread wide open, and is often said, the possibilities are endless. We hope that those who picked up the series are not to disappointed by the absence of Holmes Watson and other predominate characters o Doyle's world. Baker Street is not a pastich of Holmes nor ever intended to be. We thin our characters have a "life" of their own, an hopefully you'll agree.

Gary Reed

BAKER STREET: Children of the Night. Reprinting issues 1-5 the Baker Street series. Published by Caliber Press 11904 Farming: Rd., Livonia MI 48150. ©1993 by Guy Davis and Gary Reed. T. page artwork © their respective creators.

Written And Illustrated By
Guy Davis

CHILDREN OF THE NIGHT
ACT I
"Sisters"

Co-Creator
Gary Reed

Cover Painting
Vince Locke

Letters

Editor
Chester Jacques

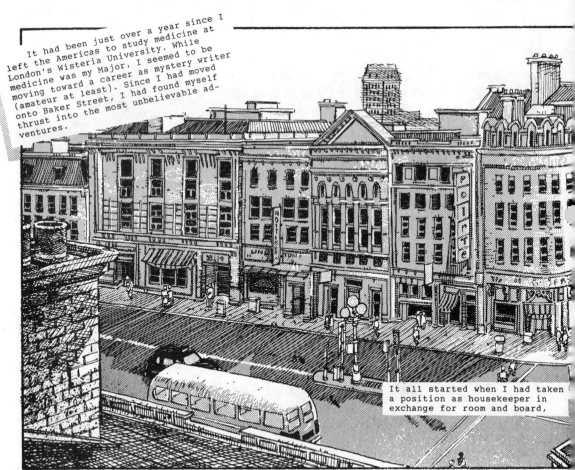

It had been just over a year since I left the Americas to study medicine at London's Wisteria University. While medicine was my Major, I seemed to be moving toward a career as mystery writer (amateur at least). Since I had moved onto Baker Street, I had found myself thrust into the most unbelievable adventures.

It all started when I had taken a position as housekeeper in exchange for room and board,

though I had never expected to be maid among the punk lifestyle of my room mates, Sharon Ford, and her girlfriend Samantha Neville.

I admit the whole punk "thing" was something I didn't understand, and in a way I guess I was afraid of it. But the more time I spent with Sharon, or "Harlequin" as most of the punks called her, the more comfortable I felt.

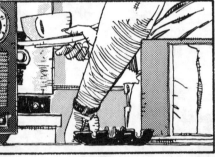

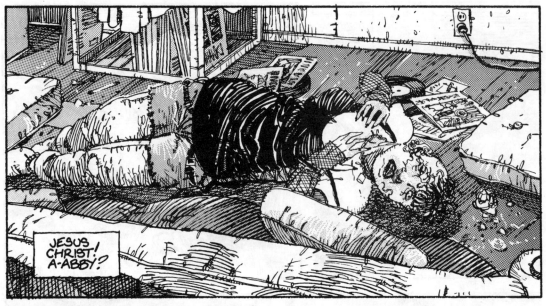

Whenever I went anywhere with Sam I was guaranteed to end up in some sort of trouble. I thought, or at least hoped, that Sam was finally starting to accept me. But just when you think you got her as a friend she turns away and makes you feel like...well, a tourist.

Of course that was only part of my worries at the moment. The whole morning seemed to flash through my head, all the question I had wanted to ask Sam. About her transvestite friends, the fight, and everything else she wouldn't tell me.

Since they locked the doors on us, she hadn't said two words. Which was odd for Sam considering her temper, but understandable as I couldn't get the face of the strangled girl out of my mind either...

TAK TAK TAK

SHARON!

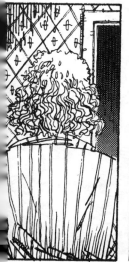

Written And Illustrated By Guy Davis

CHILDREN OF THE NIGHT
ACT II
"The Inquisition"

Co-Creator
Gary Reed

Letters
Vince Locke

Editor
Chester Jacques

SURE... I DON'T KNOW... I DON'T KNOW WHAT I SHOULD SAY TO "HER".

WHY SHOULD THIS FACT CHANGE ANYTHING?

SHE'S--HE'S A MAN WHO DRESSES UP LIKE A WOMAN! I MEAN... I DON'T CARE IF HE'S GAY, BUT--

HA HA... BELIEVE ME, SAM'S NOT GAY. YOU WOULDN'T 'AVE GUESSED SHE WAS A MAN UNLESS YOU SAW HER WITH HER SKIRT UP, SO TREAT 'ER AS SHE SEEMS.

SEXUALITY IS MORE OF A PERSONAL BELIEF THAN A SET ROLE FOR MANY. LIKE LOVE, IT'S SOMETHING YOU FEEL, NOT SOMETHING YOU LEARN FROM A BOOK. IT'S ONE OF THE FEW REAL MYSTERIES LEFT.

I DON'T KNOW, I'M NOT USED TO ALL THIS. I GUESS IT THREW ME. I WAS BEGINNING TO FEEL AT HOME. SAM'S JUST-- IT'S JUST DIFFICULT TRYING TO GET TO KNOW HER, AND SHE'S NOT HELPING MUCH LATELY. I DON'T KNOW HOW YOU PUT UP WITH HER.

SHE'S NOT ALL THAT BAD. SHE JUST NEEDS 'ER SPACE SOMETIMES...

WITH THESE RIPPER KILLINGS, I THINK WE'RE ALL ON EDGE, ESPECIALLY SAM. SHE LIVES T'GO OUT AT NIGHT, AND NOW IT'S GETTING MORE DANGEROUS.

YEAH... SO WHAT WENT ON WITH PINNER YESTERDAY? ANY CLUES OR ANYTHING?

WELL, NOW THAT YOU ASK....

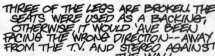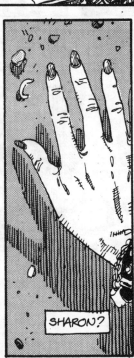

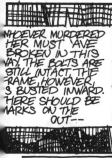

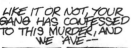

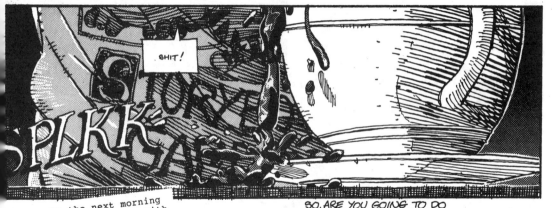

I awoke the next morning Sharon and Sam at odds with each other. Sharon, staying up most of the night with her mystery, and Sam frustrated by her preoccupation with it all.

GREAT. WAKE UP, WILL YA...

SO, ARE YOU GOING TO DO ANYTHING ABOUT THOSE "INQUISITION" GIRLS?

NOTHING. I'LL LET PINNER RUN WITH HIS INVESTIGATION. HE'LL REALIZE THEY 'AVE NO REAL INVOLVEMENT, AND LET IT GO.

AND HOPEFULLY PARKER WILL REALIZE THE SAME WITH JIM RUNAWAY ONCE I SEE THE LINK TO 'IM.

WHY BOTHER? THE ONE TIME THE LAW NICKS THE RIGHT KID, AND YOU GO DOWN TRYING TO FREE 'IM. OR IS IT THAT YOU 'AVE TO MAKE A PROBLEM ONLY YOU CAN SOLVE.

LUV, HE COULDN'T 'AVE KILLED HER. SOMEONE'S SETTING 'IM UP AND THIS LINK IS PROOF. WHY GO TO THE TROUBLE OF MURDERING SOMEONE IN A WAY THAT COULD ONLY POINT TO YOU? HE ALSO WOULDN'T BREAK THE FRONT DOOR IN IF HE KNEW TO COME IN THE WINDOW.

~ END ACT II ~

Written And Illustrated By
Guy Davis

CHILDREN OF THE NIGHT
ACT III
"London After Midnight"

Co-Creator
Gary Reed

Cover Painting
Vince Locke

Letters

Editor
Chester Jacques

I HAVEN'T STARTED MY INVESTIGATION YET. THE RAIN EARLIER ISN'T GOING TO MAKE IT ANY EASIER.

WE'RE DOWN--PLAYING IT TO THE PRESS, BUT I CAN'T BELIEVE THIS HAS HAPPENED. THERE WERE TWO OTHER BOBS AROUND THIS AREA LAST NIGHT, NEITHER 'EARD A THING. CONSTABLE RANGE FOUND HIS BODY WHEN HE REPORTED TO TAKE OVER 'IS WALK.

CHRIST.

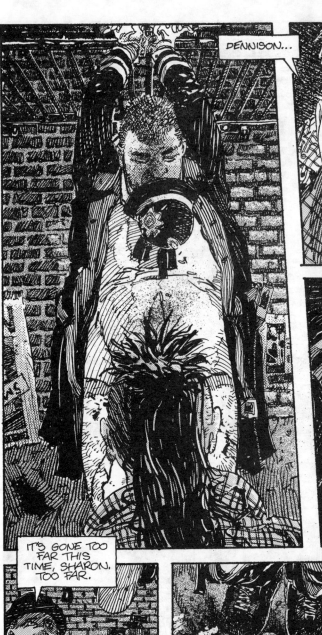

DENNISON...

IT'S GONE TOO FAR THIS TIME, SHARON. TOO FAR.

HMM, I THINK THIS SHOULD FREE THE INQUISITION OF ANY GUILT. LOOK...

"THE INQUISITION ARE... THE CHILDREN WHO WILL BE BLAMED FOR NOTHING."

WHAT? SHARON, THAT'S DENNISON UP THERE. GRAFFITI IS THE LAST THING I'M CONCERNED ABOUT.

THE RIPPER 'AS LEFT US A SIGNATURE, PINNER. THE WORDIN' ITSELF SHOULD HOLD A SIGNIFICANT CLUE.

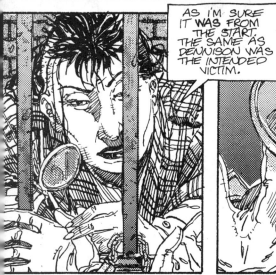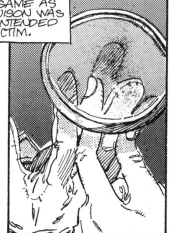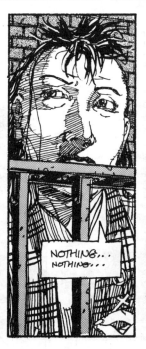

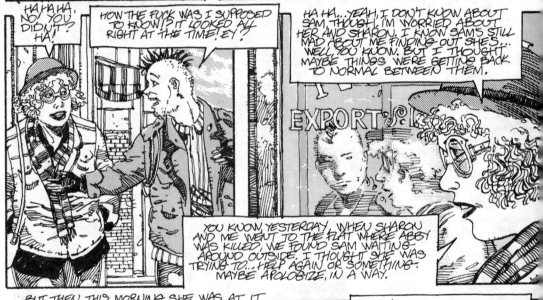

HELLO?

HELLO, SAM? THIS IS PINNER. LOOK, IS SHARON AROUND?

NO.

WHERE IS SHE?

I DON'T KNOW. I'M NOT 'ER MUM.

ALRIGHT, SAM, LOOK, TELL 'ER I CALLED. TELL HER THE LINK OF THE NECKLACE I GAVE BARKER MAY PUT JIM IN THE CLEAR FOR NOW. ALL WE 'AVE TO DO IS GET IT PAST STRAND AND HE'LL GET OUT OF 'ERE AT LEAST.

HA. FIGURES.

I'LL TRY CALLING TOMORROW. WE'LL BE GETTING THE FORENSICS ON DENNISON. IF YOU SEE HER—

I SAID I'D TELL 'ER.

CLAK

LOOK, I KNOW YOU 'AVE TO GO OUT. BE WITH YOUR "CHILDREN OF THE NIGHT" AND ALL. BUT I'M SURE THE RIPPER IS SOMEONE IN THE SCENE. SOMEONE WHO FREQUENTS THE BASKERVILLES OR KNOWS THE SURROUNDING AREA.

ALL THE VICTIMS WERE SEEN AROUND THE CLUB BEFORE THEY WERE KILLED, AND ALL THE BODIES WERE IN ALLEYS THAT LEAD FROM MARLYEBONE RD. THE RIPPER PROBABLY FOLLOWS THEM UNTIL THEY'RE ALONE, THEN...

...I'M SORRY, SAM, I'M TOO USED TO YOUR 'ELP. I DON'T MEAN TO DRAG YOU INTO THIS. I WISH THIS CASE WASN'T TAKING ALL MY ATTENTION. MAYBE THEN...

WHAT MYSTERY POUT!?

DON' APOLOGIZE FOR SOMETHING YOU'RE NOT SORRY ABOUT!

YOU DON'T NEED M'HELP! YOU'RE NOT MISSIN' ANYTHING WITHOUT ME! NOTHING AT ALL. SO DON'T PLAY THIS SHIT WITH ME!

SAM, LET'S NOT GO THROUGH THIS AGAIN, YOU KNOW I NEED YOU.

I felt odd following her but curiosity compelled me to continue unseen. I wanted to know where she had been these past days and why she had to be alone. There were a lot of questions I wanted the answers to, and I decided it was time to find them out on my own.

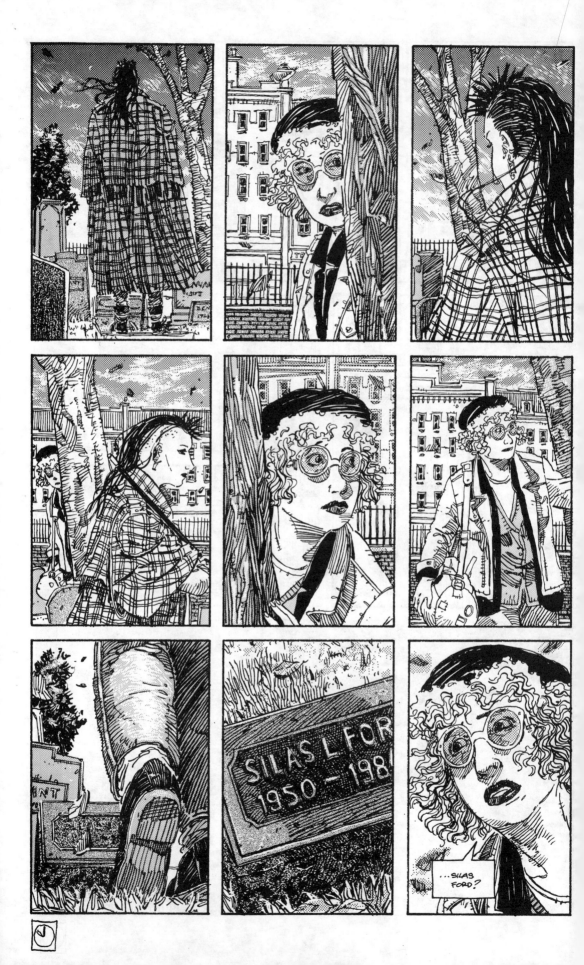

"SHARON, WHAT'S GOING ON?"

"LOOK, FROM THE START OUR ONLY CONNECTION WITH ALL THESE MURDERS WERE THAT THE ATTACKS WERE AIMED AT THE MALE GENDER. AS FOR A MOTIVE, THE FIRST TWO VICTIMS WERE CONVICTED RAPISTS WITH DRUG HABITS THAT TOOK THEM TO 'PIT ALLEY'."

"THAT MADE ME BELIEVE SEXUAL ASSAULTS WERE THE RIPPER'S TARGETS. BUT WHEN RAO WAS KILLED, I LET MYSELF BELIEVE THE MOTIVE WASN'T RELATED. LATER, I FOUND OUT THE NIGHT HE WAS KILLED, RAO 'AD GOTTEN DRUNK AND HIT HIS GIRLFRIEND AT THE CLUB."

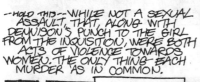

"--HOLD THIS-- WHILE NOT A SEXUAL ASSAULT, THAT, ALONG WITH DENNISON'S PUNCH TO THE GIRL FROM THE INQUISITION, WERE BOTH ACTS OF VIOLENCE TOWARDS WOMEN. THE ONLY THING EACH MURDER 'AS IN COMMON."

"SO HOW DO YOU GET JIM AS THE NEXT TARGET?"

"HE WAS WELL PUBLICIZED IN THE PRESS AS ABBY'S KILLER."

"BUT HE DIDN'T KILL HER."

"NO ONE KNOWS THAT BUT US, AND I DON'T THINK IT WOULD MATTER TO THE RIPPER. RAO'S SLAP WAS AS MUCH OF A CRIME AS RAPE. THE RIPPER CAN'T DISTINGUISH BETWEEN THE TWO."

"KNOWING THE RIPPER WOULD SURELY GO AFTER JIM, I HAD PLANNED TO USE 'IM TO LURE THE RIPPER OUT, CATCH 'ER IN THE ACT. NOW IT LOOKS LIKE THAT MAY GO AHEAD AS PLANNED, BUT NO ONE WILL BE AROUND TO STOP HIS MURDER."

"WE 'AVE TO GET TO HIM BEFORE 'E'S SEEN AT THE BASKERVILLES... BEFORE THE RIPPER KNOWS HE'S BEEN RELEASED."

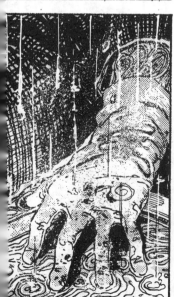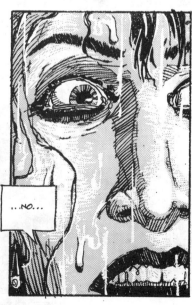

Written And Illustrated By Guy Davis

CHILDREN OF THE NIGHT
ACT IV
"Requim En Masse"

Co-Creator
Gary Reed

Cover Painting
Vince Locke

Letters

Editor
Gary Reed

A week later we buried Sam...it's still very difficult for me to understand everything I felt at the time. Shock and horror over the fact that I was so close to a... murderer. But more so, I felt a loss and sadness to someone I didn't understand but who I would also consider a friend in my memories.

My emotions worried me at the time but no more so than Sharons', I could only guess what she was going through and feel for her.

It would be the only time I would ever see her cry openly, reach out on her feelings. I could only try to give her the support she needed and promise to be there for her as I always would be.

For the woman who would always seem so strong and in control of her surroundings suddenly seemed very alone...very real.

And together the case of the "Ripper" came to a close, for us at least. To the rest of the world it would still be a mystery, the "Ripper" would never be caught. But Sam...

Sam would always be known as the last victim.

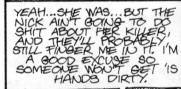

As I walked back home I began to think about Jim's case and the girl, Abby, I had found murdered. I knew it wasn't that difficult a problem for Sharon, but the memories of Sam's death had been haunting her for weeks and I worried that Sharon would never come to terms with the loss.

'ELLO, LUV.

HI, MR. HUDSON.

DID YOU GET ANY CALLERS YET?

NAY, FEEL ODD EVEN LOOKING FOR ANYONE ELSE...SHE 'AD BEEN WORKING 'ERE SINCE SHE WAS A NIPPER.

HA... YES, WELL, I'M SURE YOU'LL FIND SOMEONE.

EXPERIENCED HELP WANTED APPLY WITHIN

ERE, WAIT A MINUTE, SUSAN.

LISTEN, I 'AVEN'T BEEN UP TO SEE SHARON MUCH...Y'KNOW, WHAT WITH EVERYTHING. BUT LISTEN, YOU TELL 'ER SHE CAN STAY 'ERE AS LONG AS SHE WANTS. ON THE HOUSE. ALRIGHT?

UH, SURE... OKAY.

BUT...SILAS...HE WASN'T SO LUCKY. WHETHER IT WAS AS A WARNING TO ME OR JUST REVENGE, BEFORE MORDECAI JAMES LEFT, HE 'AD SILAS MURDERED.

HE KILLED YOUR HUSBAND...

YES, I FOUND HIM IN AN ALLEY, HIS NECK BROKEN. I...I WAS NEVER VERY GOOD WITH PERSONAL RELATIONSHIPS, BUT... I LOVED HIM MORE THAN ANYONE, EVEN MYSELF.

WITH THE LOSS OF HIM I LET MYSELF GO BACK TO THE ADDICTION THAT STARTED ALL OF THIS.

EVENTUALLY, I ENDED UP AT THE WEST END... SPENDING MY DAYS--WHAT WAS LEFT OF THEM--LYING IN PIT ALLEY, SHOOTING UP... WAITING TO DIE.

I GAVE EVERYTHING I OWNED...MYSELF...FOR MY HABIT. I 'AD MADE SOME ENEMIES OVER THE YEARS AND ENDED UP EITHER BEING CHEATED BY DEALERS OR ROLLED BY THE BOBS.

And as I slowly worked on the case of Abby Langford by myself, my mind and my worries would constantly wander back to Sharon. I wished I could understand what was going through her mind.

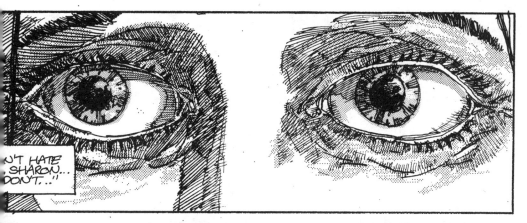

Written And Illustrated By Guy Davis

CHILDREN OF THE NIGHT

FINALE

Editor
Gary Reed

Letters
Vince Locke

Cover Painting By
Lurene Haines

Tone Assists By
Skye Gregory

It had been a couple of days since Sharon had left the apartment, overwrought and depressed over the death of her lover and our roomate Sam.

I was still, I guess, in shock over Sam's suicide, not to mention the revelation that I had been living with a murderer this past year.

A death that ended the murderous acts of the Ripper and claimed the murderers life as well.

It's still disturbing to think of to this day, how I could hate her for what she had done, but at the same time I missed her dearly.

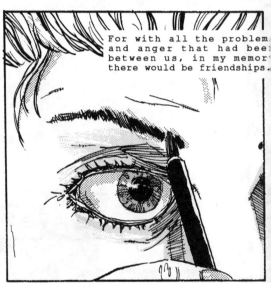

For with all the problems and anger that had been between us, in my memory there would be friendships.

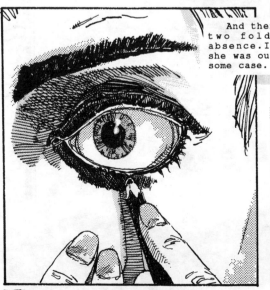

And then the loss seemed two fold with Sharons absence. I had hoped that she was out trying to solve some case.

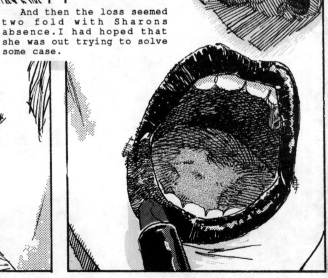

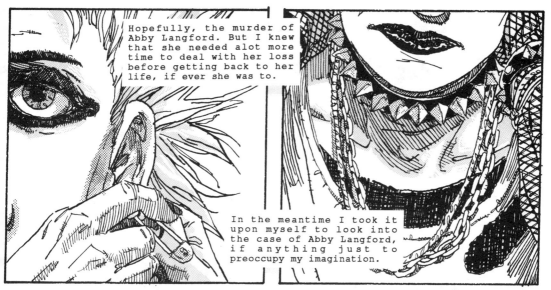

Hopefully, the murder of Abby Langford. But I knew that she needed alot more time to deal with her loss before getting back to her life, if ever she was to.

In the meantime I took it upon myself to look into the case of Abby Langford, if anything just to preoccupy my imagination.

had thought of going to the "Baskervilles" to talk about it with Jim Carnaway, the man accused of her murder. Innocent, but the only link to this case.

Of course getting into the club was next to impossible unless they knew you or you were part of some gang.

The first time I went was with Sam showing me around, this time it would be just me trying to fit into a place where you weren't suppose to fit in.

I don't know though, I still thought I looked kinda silly.

But for as imposing as the club had been, getting in was a lot easier than I thought, and it only cost me a fiver to get pass the bouncers.

Once I was inside it would take a little more to find Jim in the sea of black leather and mohawks.

"I LOVED WITH YOU I CRIED WITH YOU PROBABLY DID A LOT OF THINGS I SHOULDN'T DO"

"I LOOKED AROUND AND YOU LOOKED DOWN I GUESS THAT MAKES YOU REALIZE JUST WHAT YOU FOUN YOU GIVE ME MIXED SIGNALS ALL THE TIME MIXED SIGNALS ALL THE TIME"

"YES? WHAT IS THE PROBLEM?"

"I'M HERE WITH NEWS CONCERNING THE MURDER OF ABIGAIL LANGFORD."

"WHAT OF INSPECTOR BARKER?"

"I'M IN CHARGE OF THE INVESTIGATION NOW. PLEASE ANNOUNCE US."

"YES, WELL, HE IS VERY UPSET BY ALL AND HAS A LOT OF RESPONS--"

"THIS IS A POLICE MATTER, SIR. AND NOT ONE I AM ABOUT TO DISCUSS WITH YOU. I WILL NOT PRESS HIM FOR TIME, BUT I WILL SPEAK WITH HIM."

"NOW ANNOUNCE US, OR GET OUT OF MY WAY!"

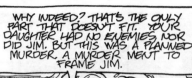

"ENOUGH! YOU MAY HAVE TALKED YOUR WAY OUT OF MY OFFICE IN THE PAST, BUT YOU DON'T HAVE THAT LUXURY THIS TIME. AND DON'T THINK FOR A MINUTE THAT I DON'T KNOW OF PINNER'S INVOLVEMENT."

"RELEASING REPORTS, FORENSICS, EVIDENCE, NOT TO MENTION ALLOWING YOU TO QUESTION THE SUSPECT IN ALL THIS."

"FOR NOW, HE IS STILL UNDER SUSPICION."

"WELL... THAT IS A MATTER FOR US TO DEAL WITH. YOU NEED TO REMEMBER YOU HAVE NO BUSINESS HERE. AND YOUR PAST ACHIEVEMENTS, SUCH AS THEY WERE, ARE REMEMBERED ONLY BY YOU."

"EVEN YOU SHOULD KNOW ENOUGH ABOUT COMMON DEDUCTION TO SEE THAT JIM CARNAWAY IS INNOCENT."

"LANGFORD SHOULD BE UNDER YOUR 'SUSPICION.' HE KNOWS WHO KILLED HIS DAUGHTER, AND IT WASN'T JIM."

"YOU HAVE LANGFORD TO THANK THAT YOU'RE ALLOWED TO WALK OUT OF HERE. HE SEEMS TO APPRECIATE YOUR VISIT AND ALL."

"STICK TO PLAYING DETECTIVE TO YOUR 'PUNKS.' THEY MAY RESPECT YOUR ABILITIES, BUT I NEVER WAS MUCH IMPRESSED."

"THINGS HAVE CHANGED A LOT SINCE YOU WERE HERE, MS. FORD. YOU'LL FIND WHAT TALENTS YOU HAVE WON'T BE MUCH USE THE WAY YOU USE THEM."

"OF COURSE, I DIDN'T WANT YOU TO LOOK BAD TO THE UPPER CLASS."

"THEN THINGS HAVEN'T CHANGED AT ALL."

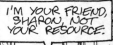

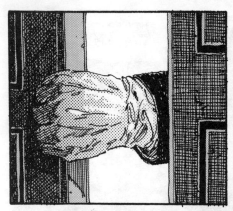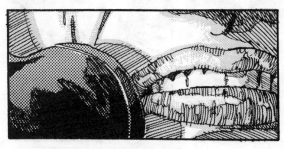

afterword

When I started work on Baker Street, Sam's role and fate was planned at the beginning. Halfway through the first mystery she started to become the readers' favorite character and I had the dubious task of killing her off. The biggest question to everyone was why she did it and why she had to die? Something I didn't want to explain fully, the story wasn't about mystery and motives as it was about Sharon and Sam.

With the first mystery to the series "Honour Among Punks," I wanted to set up the traditional mystery story, complete with the final battle. With "Children of the Night" I always intended it to be anti-climatic. I wanted a story that built up to a big confrontation... that never happened. It wasn't about good and evil, but misunderstandings and pain, and the frailties in us all.

Guy Davis

Portrait by Bob Monks 1989, Revised for 1993

appendium

Pages 162-165
Advertising artwork for the "Children of the Night" storyline.

Page 166
Swimsuit illustration for the "Amazing Heroes Swimsuit Special." (1991)

Page 167
Commissioned illustration of Sam.

Pages 168-175
Artwork for the BAKER STREET Calendar, never completed.

BAKER STREET

"...the cobblestone will run red..."

Children Of The Night

Written/Illustrated
by Guy Davis

Painted Covers by Vince Locke

A new four-part mystery
from Caliber Press

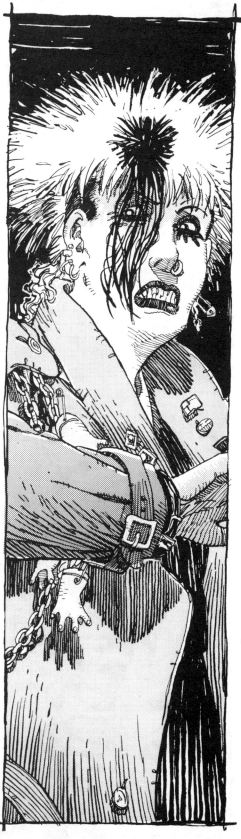